THE *Berenstain* BEAR SCOUTS

and the
Really Big
Disaster

Look for more books in
The Berenstain Bear Scouts series:

THE Berenstain BEAR SCOUTS
and the
Really Big Disaster

by Stan & Jan Berenstain
Illustrated by Michael Berenstain

A
LITTLE APPLE
PAPERBACK

SCHOLASTIC INC.
New York Toronto London Auckland Sydney

ISBN 0-590-94481-9

12 11 10 9 8 7 6 5 4 3 2 1   8 9/9 0 1 2 3/0

Printed in the U.S.A.   40

First Scholastic printing, March 1998

• Table of Contents •

and the
Really Big
Disaster

• Chapter 1 •

The Great Creature Stirs

It was morning. The rising sun was beginning to take the chill off the Great Grizzly Mountains. An enormous creature was beginning to stir in a cave near the top of the tallest peak in the range.

It was Bigpaw, of course. Bigpaw was the gigantic bear whom Professor Actual Factual and the Bear Scouts had discovered on a fossil hunt. A "living fossil" Actual Factual had called him. And "fossil" he was — a throwback to the prehistoric cavebears who had roamed the earth with the saber-toothed tiger, the woolly mammoth, and the giant ground sloth. And "living" he certainly was. Not only living, but *bigger* than life. Much, *much* bigger. He had legs like tree trunks, shoulders like boulders, and paws like Dumpsters. At first sight Bigpaw was terrifying — at second and third sight, too.

But after a while it became clear that despite his great size and stupendous strength, Bigpaw was a gentle, sweet-natured fellow. He was especially fond of his discoverers, the professor and the Bear Scouts. Having discovered Bigpaw, they felt a certain responsibility toward the big fellow. The scouts visited him from time to time. They even brought him presents. The big teddy that Bigpaw slept with had been a hibernation gift from the scouts. The professor's main interest in Bigpaw was scientific. But as Actual Factual did his Bigpaw research, he came to think of

the big fellow as a friend rather than a research object.

But as Bigpaw rose from his bed of straw, brush, and moss, he did not seem his old happy self. It had been days since he had wakened with a smile. Lately, he had been stirring from his bed feeling . . . well, sort of sad. This feeling of sadness seemed to be getting worse. He wondered about it. But while Bigpaw was good at moving boulders, ripping up trees by their roots, and stopping avalanches, he wasn't very good at wondering. He tried. But the more he wondered about why he was sad, the sadder he got.

Now Bigpaw was out of his bed. As he brushed bits of bedstraw from his thick fur, he looked toward the bright, sunny opening of his cave. Sunshine usually made Bigpaw feel happy. But not today. Now he was out on the cave ledge feeling the warmth of the sun. The warmth of the sun usually made him feel happy. But not today.

Then, as Bigpaw looked far across the valley at Beartown, something happened in his mind. As he looked across the valley at busy Beartown's houses, stores, and factories, and the farms and forests that surrounded them, Bigpaw had a twinkling of why he was sad. Perhaps it was more a feeling than a thought. But whatever it was, it told him what he had to do. He started down the mountain.

• Chapter 2 •

A Good Shaking

"Yuck!" said Scout Sister.

"I can't look!" said Scout Lizzy.

"Please," said Scout Brother. "Actual Factual isn't dissecting the frog for fun."

"That's right," said Fred, the fourth member of the "one-for-all-and-all-for-one!" scout troop. "Frogs are dying all over the place. The professor is trying to find out why."

"Yuck, nevertheless," said Sister.

"I still can't look," said Lizzy.

The scouts were the ones who had brought the dead frog to Professor Actual

Factual. Besides being the foremost scientist of his time, Actual Factual was director of the Bearsonian Institution, Bear Country's most important museum.

"Do you think it's some kind of pollution?" asked Brother.

"Possibly," said the professor. "But I won't be able to say for sure until I do some te—"

But before he could get the word "tests" out, the whole museum began to shake.

"The fault! It's broken loose!" cried the professor. He ran to a machine that was noisily cranking out paper. The machine was the seismograph that the professor always kept plugged in because of the fault that lay under Beartown. Great Grizzly Fault it was called.

"I don't understand!" cried the professor as the shaking got worse. "It's only a three on the Richter scale, but it *feels* like a six."

But Brother had a feeling about the shaking. He opened the lab door and looked across the lobby at the entrance. "It's not an earthquake, professor!" cried Brother. "It's Bigpaw!"

Bigpaw's muzzle was poking through the doorway. Not only were the double doors splintered and off their hinges, the stonework and the framing were crumbling.

It was clear to Brother what had happened: Bigpaw had knocked on the front door and, failing to get the professor's attention, had given the Bearsonian a bit of a shaking.

"Hi, Bigpaw," said Brother. "What seems to be the problem?"

"Bigpaw have big problem," answered the biggest bear of them all. "Bigpaw need help. Bigpaw need to talk to professor."

"Bless my spectacles!" cried the professor when he saw the condition of the entrance. As kindly as the professor was, it was clear that he was about to reprimand Bigpaw severely.

"Er, easy, professor," cautioned Brother.

"Easy?" said the professor, with fire in his eyes.

"It seems, professor," said Brother, "that Bigpaw is in some kind of trouble. He's come to you for advice."

"Oh," said the professor, recovering his kindly tone. "In that case, Bigpaw, come right in."

"No!" shouted the Bear Scouts.

"He's already wrecked the entrance," said Brother. "Do you want him to wreck the whole Bearsonian?"

"Of course," said the professor, who was as absentminded as he was kindly. "Tell you what, scouts. You take our friend around to the parking lot. We'll discuss his problem outdoors."

Bigpaw looked upset. "I sorry I break

door. I fix it!" So saying, he began to gather up the doors, the stonework, and the framing.

"No!" cried Brother. "You'll only make it worse!"

"Er, yes," said the professor. "I'll get Gus, my bear of all work, to fix the door — after all, that's his job. I'll cut through the museum and meet you out back."

• Chapter 3 •

A Job for Bigpaw?

There was more than a parking lot behind
the museum. There was the huge hangar
that housed Saucer One, the professor's
combination flying saucer, balloon, and
submarine. There was his sciencemobile, a
van that was fitted out to do almost any
kind of science. The professor was not only
the director of the Bearsonian, he was a
physicist, a chemist, a biologist, an an-
thropologist, a botanist, and a psycholo-
gist. But for all his achievements in those
fields, the professor was best known for
his discovery of the Bear Theory of Rela-

tivity, which states that, way back when, all bears were relatives.

You couldn't have a conversation with Bigpaw the way you could with someone close to your own size. But the professor and the Bear Scouts managed. They stood up on the high ground where Actual Factual grew experimental plants. Bigpaw sat on a big boulder on the brick terrace of the museum.

"All right, Bigpaw, what seems to be the problem?" asked the professor.

"That what Bigpaw want," said Bigpaw.

Puzzled looks from the professor and the Bear Scouts. "*What's* what Bigpaw wants?" asked the professor.

"What Gus has," said Bigpaw.

"But what does Gus have that you want?" asked Sister.

"And the professor and Farmer Ben and Chief Bruno. They have one, too," said Bigpaw.

"Hmm," said the professor, beginning to lose his patience. "But what *is* it that Gus, Farmer Ben, and Chief Bruno have that you don't?"

THAT THE WORD! JOB!

Bigpaw hung his head and looked embarrassed. "Bigpaw forget word," he said.

Actual Factual looked at the Bear Scouts and shrugged. The scouts shrugged back. There was a long silence.

Then Fred said, "Wait a minute. Remember back when Bigpaw started to fix the entrance and we said Gus would do it because it was his *job*?"

"That the word! Job!" cried Bigpaw, jumping up and down and shaking the Bearsonian all over again. "Bigpaw want job! Bigpaw want be — want be —" The big fellow was clearly reaching for a word he couldn't find.

"Useful? Is that it?" said Lizzy.

"That right!" cried the giant. "Bigpaw want be . . . useful!"

Good grief, thought the big fellow's friends. Bigpaw wants to be useful.

• Chapter 4 •

Aptitude Testing

Bigpaw was smiling from ear to ear —
and since Bigpaw's ears were about
twenty-two inches apart, that was a
pretty big smile. Bigpaw felt a great sense
of relief. It hadn't been easy, but he had
somehow managed to tell his friends what
his problem was. It was as if an enormous
weight had been lifted off his shoulders.

Not so the professor and the Bear
Scouts. They felt as if an enormous weight
had been *placed* on their shoulders. A job
for Bigpaw? Why not a job for a tornado, a
job for a hurricane, a job for thunder and

lightning? While Bigpaw smiled from ear to ear, Actual Factual and the scouts huddled.

"Poor guy. He hasn't got a clue!" said Fred.

"Whew! Talk about mission impossible!" said Sister.

"But we've got to help him," said Lizzy.

"But how?" said Brother. "I just don't see how he can fit into the modern world of work."

"Everything is technology today," said Fred.

"And he can't even read," said Sister.

"But there must be something he can do," said Brother.

Professor Actual Factual, who had been silent, finally spoke. "Aptitude tests," said the professor.

"What kind of tests?" said Scout Sister.

"Aptitude tests," said the professor. "They're tests you give to find out what kind of job somebody is suited for. Fred, would you please explain to Bigpaw while I organize the tests?" Actual Factual went into the Bearsonian.

"Where professor go?" asked Bigpaw. "He find job for Bigpaw?"

"Not exactly, big fella. But it's going to be okay," said Brother. "You've come to the right place. The professor is a job expert."

"He's going to give you some tests to find out just what sort of job you're suited for," said Fred.

The professor returned with a whole wheelbarrow of test things. It was quite a

collection. First there was a shape-sorter test. There was a thick steel plate with a hole in it and a dozen oddly shaped rods. Of the dozen rods, only one would fit through the hole. The object of the test was to see how long it took Bigpaw to select the right rod and push it through the hole. The second was an object-matching test. Bigpaw would be given six objects: an iron bar, a jar of mustard, a magnet, a log, a soft pretzel, and a saw. The object of the test was to see how long it took Bigpaw to match the iron bar with the magnet, the pretzel with the mustard, and the saw with the log.

Bigpaw listened carefully as the professor explained the tests. Then, at the word "Go!" he went through those tests like a hot knife through butter. First he pushed — not one — but *all* the oddly shaped steel rods through the hole in the steel plate. It took some doing, but he did it. Next, he bent the iron bar into a pretzel. Then he picked up the saw with the magnet, bent the magnet into an earring, and put it on. Finally, he smeared the log with mustard and ate it.

Actual Factual and the Bear Scouts were stunned. Bigpaw's performance was a real jaw-dropper.

"Well?" said Bigpaw. "How Bigpaw do?"

The professor was speechless. His tests were all bent out of shape. The professor was pretty bent out of shape himself. "My tests!" he cried. "They're ruined!"

"Maybe so, professor," said Brother. "But they've done the job. They've told us what Bigpaw's strengths are! Bigpaw's strengths are *strength, strength,* and more *strength*! So all we have to do is find a job that calls for mighty mammoth muscular strength!"

"It's got to be outdoors, of course," said Sister.

"Wait a minute! I think I have an idea!" said Brother. "What sort of hired bear do you think Bigpaw would make?"

"A magnificent hired bear!" cried the rest of the troop.

"A brilliant idea!" said the professor. "Come, let's go see Farmer Ben. This way, Bigpaw. We think we have a job for you."

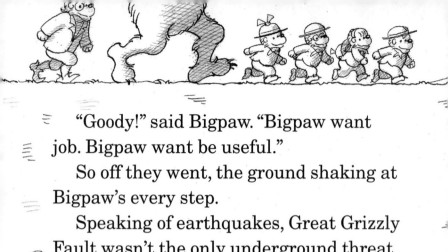

"Goody!" said Bigpaw. "Bigpaw want job. Bigpaw want be useful."

So off they went, the ground shaking at Bigpaw's every step.

Speaking of earthquakes, Great Grizzly Fault wasn't the only underground threat to the bears. There was Weaselworld, the secret underground network of tunnels, caves, offices, workshops, laboratories, and factories ruled by Weasel McGreed, sworn enemy of the bears, who had vowed to take over Bear Country lock, stock, and honeypot.

• Chapter 5 •
A Change of Policy

At the very moment when job seeker Big-paw and company were approaching Farmer Ben's farm, Weasel McGreed, evil genius, master of all weasels, was about to announce an important change of policy. Present in McGreed's cavelike office were the members of his inner council. There

was General Maxx, commander of the weasel armies; Dr. Boffins, Weaselworld's chief scientist; and Stye, a tunnel tough who had come up the hard way and was McGreed's chief henchweasel. Even though they were VIWs (Very Important Weasels), they felt like middle-schoolers called to the principal's office.

You couldn't blame them for being nervous. McGreed had a terrible temper. He had once demoted General Maxx to corporal for leaving a button unbuttoned. And once when Dr. Boffins forgot to say "Sir," McGreed had taken his Bunsen burner away. And he had forced Stye to push a peanut through the endless tunnels of Weaselworld with his nose just for the heck of it. So it's no wonder that the members of the inner council were sweating under the yellow-eyed gaze of Weasel McGreed. What made it worse was the weasely little smile that curled his crooked mouth.

"Please relax, my friends," said Mc-Greed.

Please relax, my friends? Was it possible? Could this be the Weasel McGreed whom they knew so well and were terrified of?

"Surprised, aren't you?" said McGreed. "The fact is, I'm a new weasel. I've turned over an entirely new leaf." The members of the council began to relax — just a little. "And I owe it all to this book." McGreed held up the book. It was called *How to Win Friends and Influence Weasels.* "You're looking at the new calm McGreed who does not allow himself to be eaten up by anger, who keeps his anger under control."

The members of the council began to relax a little more. McGreed's eyes got a little narrower. "Not that I don't have reason to be angry. Indeed, I have ample reason to be angry. As you know, it is my sworn goal to take over Bear Country lock, stock, and honeypot. And, as you well know, my efforts to achieve that goal have not been successful. The failure of my humongous pumpkin scheme was especially galling. Ditto the failure of my sci-fi pizza scheme." McGreed's smile was beginning to fade. The members of the council began to tense up — just a little.

"But that's all water over the dam," continued McGreed. "Or is it water under the bridge? Which is it, General Maxx? Over the dam or under the bridge?"

"Er, I b-b-b-believe either is acceptable, sir," said the general.

"I don't want to know what you believe, you pinheaded, bacteria-brained numskull, I want to know *which* it is!" No more smiles. Control had given way to wild-eyed spit-flying anger. "So get this through your hollow heads. I'm announcing a new policy. No more 'taking over' Bear Coun-

try! No more Mr. Nice Guy! The new policy
is to destroy Bear Country! So get out of
here and bring me back a plan that will
destroy Bear Country lock, stock, and honeypot!"

McGreed sank back into his chair. "Dismissed," he said.

The members of the council just stared.

"Didn't you hear me, you idiots? DIS-
MISSED!"

• Chapter 6 •

Bigpaw's Job "Interview"

"You can't be serious," said Farmer Ben.

"We're dead serious," said the professor. The Bear Scouts nodded in agreement.

"Let's see if I understand this," said Ben. "You want me to take that big fellow on as a hired bear?"

"Exactly," said Brother.

"I dunno," said Ben. He went over to the window. Mrs. Ben joined him. Bigpaw was sitting on a huge pile of hay bales, waiting patiently. "He's mighty big," said Ben.

"And mighty strong," said Fred.

Ben's farm animals had come to stare at the great creature. "Hello, chickens," said Bigpaw. "Hello, sheep. Hello, piggies."

"He seems gentle enough," said Mrs. Ben.

"Gentle as a lamb," said Sister.

"What's it gonna cost me?" asked Ben.

"Regular hired bear wages," said the professor. "Bigpaw isn't about money."

"Not about money?" said Ben. "Then what's he wanna be a hired bear for?"

"He just wants a job. He's lonesome out there in the mountains," said Brother. "He just wants to feel useful."

"That's sweet," said Mrs. Ben.

"How am I gonna feed him?" asked Ben. "I can't have him going after my crops. He'll eat me out of house and farm in no time."

"Not a problem," said Brother. "He'll feed off the wild woods over there."

"That woods is nothing but junk trees,

brambles, and skunk cabbage," said Ben.

"Perfect," said Fred. "Bigpaw's system needs a lot of roughage."

"Can't use him in the winter," said Ben.

"Bigpaw hibernates in the winter," said Lizzy.

"I dunno," said Ben.

"For Pete's sake," said Mrs. Ben. "That's enough hemming and hawing and I-dunno-ing! The least you can do is give the big fella a chance to show what he can do."

Since Ben couldn't think of any more questions, he led the way out of the house, over to where Bigpaw was waiting pa-tiently on the huge stack of hay bales.

"Well," said the professor, "what would you like Bigpaw to do?"

"Lemme see now," said Ben.

"How about havin' him move those hay bales to the barn and put 'em in the loft?" suggested Mrs. Ben.

"Fair enough," said Ben. "Big fella,

those hay bales you're sittin' on: I want
you to move 'em over to the barn and
put 'em through that little second-story
window."

Bigpaw stood up, looked at the hay bales, and looked at the window. Then he put his shoulder into the whole stack and pushed it a hundred yards over to the barn and started putting the bales into the window one by one. Ben was impressed. It would have taken him two days and a hired hoist to do what Bigpaw had done in minutes.

"Well," said the professor, "is he hired?"

Before Ben could say "I dunno" again, Mrs. Ben let out a terrified scream. "The bull is loose! Run for your life!"

Blue Blazes, Ben's ferocious prize bull, was out of his pen and charging. All present ran for their lives: Ben, Mrs. Ben, the

professor, the scouts, the chickens, the sheep, and the pigs. Everyone except Big-paw. He simply stood his ground, plucked up the bull in one of his Dumpster-sized paws, carried the cowering bull back to his pen, and locked the gate.

"He's hired," said Ben.

• Chapter 7 •

It's All a Matter of Calculation

With Dr. Boffins in the lead, the members of Weaselworld's inner council were headed back to the inner sanctum of the terrible-tempered Weasel McGreed. Dr. Boffins was in the lead for two reasons. First, the plan for the destruction of Bear Country was his, and second, General Maxx and Stye were even more frightened of Weasel McGreed than Dr. Boffins was. The door guard conducted them into Mc-Greed's cavelike office. McGreed was pacing. Not a good sign.

"Sit," said McGreed. The three sat. "I

take it you have devised a plan for the complete and total destruction of Bear Country."

Dr. Boffins stood. "Yessir," he said.

"Speak," said McGreed.

Dr. Boffins spoke. "In exploring the idea of the complete and total destruction of Bear Country, I found that there are only four forces powerful enough to achieve the desired result. They are flood, tornado, hurricane, and earthquake."

McGreed stopped pacing and sat at his massive desk. Boffins had his full attention. "Flood's good," said McGreed. "A wall of water destroying everything in its path."

"Indeed so, sir," said Dr. Boffins. "But, given the geography of the area, there's no way I can trigger a flood that would more than get Bear Country's feet wet."

McGreed looked a little let down. But he had a lot of confidence in Dr. Boffins.

"Okay," he said. "I can live with a tornado. A great black vortex sucking up everything in its path like the mother of all vacuum cleaners."

"Would that it were possible, sir," said Dr. Boffins. "I could trigger a tornado, and while a tornado can be very destructive, its narrow path leaves much to be desired."

"Okay, no tornado," said McGreed. Stye and the general were beginning to look a little nervous.

"But, hey, hurricane has a nice ring to it," said McGreed. "Thunder and lightning, howling winds, sheeting rain — leaving Bear Country a wet, sodden mess."

"Quite so, sir," said Dr. Boffins. "But my studies show that forces involved in a hurricane are so complicated that it is beyond my power to create one."

McGreed leaned forward. His eyes narrowed to yellow slits, his needle-sharp fangs gleamed in the gloom. "Which means," snarled McGreed, "that you'd better get lucky with earthquake because if you let me down . . ."

"Luck has nothing to do with it, sir," said Dr. Boffins. "It's all a matter of calculation. As you know, the Great Grizzly Fault runs directly under Beartown. So it's just a matter of locating the trigger spot and . . ."

"Boffins," said McGreed, his eyes aglow, "if you bring this off . . ."

"There's no 'if' about it, sir," said Dr. Boffins. "As I said, it's all a matter of calculation."

• Chapter 8 •

Trouble at the Farm

It was the next day. Actual Factual and
the scouts were returning from a quick
trip to the river. They had taken some water samples and checked on some of the
ground cover the professor had planted on
the steep riverbank. No sooner had Actual
Factual pulled the sciencemobile to a stop
in the museum parking lot than Gus was
at the door waving a phone and shouting,
"Farmer Ben on the phone! He says it's ur-
gent!"

The professor hopped out of the van
and hurried to take the call. The scouts

couldn't make out what Ben was saying, but they could hear him shouting. He was shouting so loud that the professor had to hold the phone away from his ear. The professor managed to get a couple of words in edgewise. "Yes. Yes, Ben. We'll be right over!"

"What's the problem, professor?" asked Brother as the scouts followed Actual Factual back to the sciencemobile.

"Ben wouldn't say. He said I had to see it to believe it!"

The professor burned rubber pulling out of the parking lot and broke all records getting to Ben's farm. They hardly recognized the place when they got there. When they'd left the day before, Ben's farm was as neat as a pin. Not so today.

"Good grief!" cried Sister. "It looks like it's been hit by a tornado!"

Yeah, thought Brother, a tornado named Bigpaw. Some fence was ripped up, trees were uprooted, and *what in the world had happened to the barn?* It looked as if a tornado had lifted the roof off and set it on the ground. Ditto the silo, except that its roof was simply tipped up like a hat.

Farmer Ben was running down the front path raving like a maniac. Bigpaw was off in the back meadow sitting beside a tree, looking sad. Mrs. Ben was *in* the tree, talking calmly to the big fellow. But there was nothing calm about Ben. He was yelling at the top of his lungs. "Worst mistake I ever made! Look at what that monster did to my farm!"

"Yes, we see," said the professor.

"You ain't seen nothin' yet!" cried Ben. "Come look at my orchard!"

The professor and the scouts followed Ben around behind the barn. The entire orchard — trees, apples, roots, grass, and all — had been ripped out of the ground. How could it have happened? What could have gone wrong? The only feedback they were getting from Ben was screaming and hollering.

But a little later they were all seated around Mrs. Ben's kitchen table. She told them the whole story.

"The big fella started off fine," said Mrs. Ben. "He pushed the hay bales over to the barn. Then he started to put the bales into the loft window. But he got tired of puttin' 'em in one by one. So he simply lifted the roof off and dumped the bales into the barn all at once. The same with filling up the silo with corn."

"But the orchard?" said Brother. "What happened there?"

"We've been having a terrible choke-vine problem," said Mrs. Ben. "Vines as thick as your arm choking the apple trees. So we said to Bigpaw — this one's as much our fault as Bigpaw's — how about pulling out those choke vines. . . . Well, you saw the result." Mrs. Ben sighed.

"Tell 'em about the bull," said Farmer Ben. "Tell 'em about the bull!"

"Well," said Mrs. Ben, "that little run-in with Bigpaw turned the bull into a shivering, shaking mess. He just hides in his shed all day. And that messed up the cows. They like to come by and nuzzle Blue Blazes through the fence. They miss him, and it's stopped their milk."

"What's the bottom line to all this?" asked Brother.

"The bottom line," said Ben, "is *he's fired!*"

"I'll go tell him," said Mrs. Ben. "I want to let him down easy."

But Bigpaw didn't need to be told. He'd taken off down the road in the direction of the mountains.

The professor and the scouts jumped into the van and took off after him. "Wait, Bigpaw! Wait! Maybe we can find you another job!"

• Chapter 9 •

E-Day Minus Three

It was E-Day minus three. McGreed and Dr. Boffins were standing deep underground in a rough-hewn cave. Before them was a wall of rock. On the wall was a big painted X. Dr. Boffins was telling what would happen on E-Day. He was telling about how ten of the strongest weasels in Weaselworld would lift a huge battering ram. Starting slowly, they would begin to run. They would run faster and faster. Then, with a final burst of speed, they would strike the X just so. If they didn't strike it just so, the force of the earthquake would be directed down instead of up and Weaselworld would be destroyed. But if they struck the X just so, it would be Bear Country that would be destroyed. The earth would open up. Buildings would collapse. Downtown Beartown would disappear. No more Burger Bear. No more Pizza Shack. Gas mains would burst. Sewers would explode. "Beartown, which is at the exact epicenter, will be rubble. It will be the end of Bear Country as we know it."

"Tell it again," said McGreed.

"But, sir," said Dr. Boffins, "I've already told it to you three times."

"Tell it again," said McGreed.

Dr. Boffins told it again.

• Chapter 10 •

Cancel the Brainstorm

"Look," said Brother as they drove along Mountain Road. "I don't think we should follow Bigpaw this way."

"But he's so sad," said Lizzy.

"We have to cheer him up," said Sister.

"The only thing that's going to cheer him up is a job," said Brother.

"Yes," said Fred. "But who's going to hire him? The news that he's destroyed Ben's farm is bound to get around."

The professor, who had been silent, pulled to a stop and began to turn around.

"Why are you turning around?" asked Sister.

"Because I think Brother's right," said the professor. "The only thing that's going to cheer the big fellow up is a job. So let's go back to the museum and have a brainstorming session."

"Brainstorming session?" said Sister.

"It's where you sit around and try to solve a problem by exchanging ideas," said Fred.

"I think it's going to take more than a brainstorm to find Bigpaw another job," said Sister.

"Oh, my goodness!" cried Actual Factual when the Bearsonian came into view.

"What's wrong, professor?" asked Brother.

What was wrong was that Lady Grizzly's purple limo was parked in front of the museum.

"What is wrong," said the professor,

"is that I completely forgot my meeting with Lady Grizzly!"

"Uh-oh!" said Sister.

"You've got two choices, professor," said Brother. "You can go in and face her, or you can leave town and start over under another name."

Lady Grizzly was married to Squire Grizzly, the richest bear in Bear Country. He owned the Grizzly National Bank, the Grizzly Supermarket chain, Grizzly Software, WGRIZ — the local television station — the Grizzly Construction Company, and the Grizzly Movie chain. Lady Grizzly, who was a good friend of the scouts and the professor, was not someone to be kept waiting.

"She's in your office, professor," said Gus, who was still working on the entrance. "Been waiting for more than a half hour."

"Oh, dear!" said the professor. He rushed to his office. The scouts followed.

"Professor," said Lady Grizzly in a voice she saved for when she was very angry. "I've been cooling my heels so long they're numb. And while I know you're a genius and therefore absentminded, there's such a thing as too much of a bad thing. So unless you have a dazzling excuse for being late, I'm going to drop you and the Bearsonian like a bad habit."

The professor was so upset he could hardly speak. Brother came to the rescue. "I don't know how dazzling it is, but our excuse is that Bigpaw has a serious problem and we were trying to help him."

"Oh?" said Lady Grizzly. "You mean that charming living fossil fellow you discovered in the mountains? What sort of problem could someone that big and strong possibly have?"

"That's the problem," said Fred. "He's *too* strong."

"But how can that possibly be?" asked Lady Grizzly. "Please explain."

"Well, it's a long story," said Brother.

"I prefer short," said Lady Grizzly.

So the scouts and the professor pitched in and told about Bigpaw's job situation: the disaster at Ben's farm, the frightened bull, the stopped milk, the torn-up orchard, the beat-up barn.

"Oh, the poor thing," said Lady Grizzly. "He must have felt awful."

"He sure did," said Lizzy. "He was so upset he just headed back to the mountains."

"We followed him to try to cheer him up," said Sister.

"But we decided that the only way to

cheer him up was to find him another job," said Brother.

"What are you going to do about it?" asked Lady Grizzly.

"We came back here to have a brainstorming session about another job for Bigpaw," said the professor.

"But it isn't going to be easy," said Fred. "He's as strong as a hundred regular bears. He's just too strong for a job, I guess."

"Nonsense!" said Lady Grizzly. "Cancel that session because I have a job for Bigpaw — the *perfect* job."

"That's great, Lady Grizzly," said Brother. "Just what did you have in mind?"

Lady Grizzly could tell from their faces that they didn't believe her. But that didn't stop Lady Grizzly. "Have you heard of Great Grizzly Plaza?" she asked.

"Of course," said Brother. "Everybody has."

Great Grizzly Plaza was the biggest project in the history of Bear Country. It was being built by the Grizzly Construction Company, Squire Grizzly, President. When completed, Great Grizzly Plaza would cover four downtown Beartown blocks. It would have a hotel, a forty-six-plex movie theater, a sports stadium, and lots of fancy shops. It had been under way for quite a while.

"Not to tell tales out of school," said Lady Grizzly, "but Bigpaw's not the only

one with a problem. The squire is having a
terrible problem with the Great Grizzly
Plaza project. He's way behind schedule.
And he's way, way over budget."

"Over budget?" said Sister.

"That just means it's costing too much,"
said Lady Grizzly. "Now, it seems to me

that if Bigpaw and the squire could trade problems, everybody's problem would be solved." Lady Grizzly looked very pleased with herself. But the Bear Scouts and the professor just looked puzzled.

"Trade problems?" said Fred.

"Sure," said Lady Grizzly. "The squire could solve Bigpaw's problem by giving him a job. Bigpaw could solve the squire's problem by doing the work of a hundred bears." Lady Grizzly could tell the scouts and the professor weren't convinced. "Look," she said. "Don't think of Bigpaw as a construction worker. Think of him as a combination cherry picker, derrick, hoist, bulldozer, steamroller, power shovel, and dump truck."

"Do you think Squire Grizzly will go for the idea?" asked Sister.

"There's only one way to find out," said Lady Grizzly.

• Chapter 11 •

Another Job for Bigpaw

It was touch-and-go with Bigpaw. The scouts didn't know if Bigpaw would even come out of his cave. It was Lady Grizzly's purple limo that did it. Bigpaw thought it was beautiful, which it was.

"Pretty automobile," said Bigpaw.

"Thank you, Bigpaw," said Lady Grizzly. "But I'm here to talk business. I've got a job for you over at Grizzly Construction Company. Is it a deal?"

Bigpaw scratched his head. "Bigpaw want job," he said. "But Bigpaw too strong. Bigpaw hurt Ben's farm."

"No shilly-shallying, please," said Lady Grizzly. "Do you want the job or not?"

"Bigpaw want job," said the big fellow.

"Well, that's settled. Now let's go see the squire."

"Do I hear you correctly?" said the squire. "You want me to hire that Bigpaw fellow as a *construction worker*? Please! This is a business, not a charity. I'm in serious trouble on this project; I'm behind schedule and over budget. Now, if you good folks will excuse me, I've got work to do."

"Charity has nothing to do with it. This is strictly a business proposition," said Lady Grizzly. "Bigpaw will save you time and money."

"Tell me more," said the squire.

"Bigpaw has the carrying power of a six-wheeler, the lifting power of a derrick, and the digging power of a steam shovel,"

said Lady Grizzly. "And he can replace a hundred regular construction workers."

"Hmm," said the squire, thinking about how much money he would save. "Okay, where is this time-saving, money-saving miracle worker?"

Bigpaw was right outside the squire's construction office. He had followed the

purple limo in from the mountains. Bigpaw looked out over the Great Grizzly Plaza construction site. It was very exciting. Enormous foundation holes were being dug, concrete was being poured, the steel skeleton of the hotel-to-be was being erected, the floor of the unfinished stadium was being steamrolled. As far as Bigpaw was concerned, working on the Great Grizzly Plaza project would be job heaven.

• Chapter 12 •

E-Day Minus Two

Dr. Boffins and his earthquake crew had been working overtime. They had found the ten strongest weasels in Weaselworld to handle the battering ram. They were practicing even now under the watchful eye of General Maxx. Rock samples were being taken for further study at the Weaselworld laboratories. A grandstand was being built for the Very Important Weasels who would watch the event. E-Day was going to be the biggest day of Weasel McGreed's life. A special throne was being built for him. Stye was on the phone with his chief on an hour-by-hour basis. A countdown booth had been built at the rear of the earthquake room. Dr. Boffins was doing some final calculations.

• Chapter 13 •

Bigpaw, Destruction Worker

At first, Bigpaw seemed to fit right in on his new job. There were mountains of building materials at the building site: steel rods, concrete blocks, piles of lumber, coils of cable, great steel girders. The squire's foreman, Otto McFurback, started Bigpaw on moving these heavy materials to where they were needed: tons of brick, vats of mortar, truckloads of flooring material.

As Bigpaw gained confidence, he began doing things on his own. The first real trouble came when Bigpaw observed that wheelbarrowing the cement from the cement mixer to where it was being poured into wooden forms was a very slow process. Bigpaw figured it would save a lot of time if he ripped the mixer off its truck and used it like a pitcher to fill the forms. So that's what he did. It saved a lot of time, but it didn't go over so well with the owner of the rented cement-mixer truck.

"My truck! My truck!" cried the owner. "That monster has destroyed it!"

The squire's foreman calmed him down. But it *was* a great time-saver. The foreman suggested that instead of tearing the mixer off the truck, he pick up the whole truck and use *it* like a pitcher. Now Bigpaw was really into the swing of things. When the job came to a stop because they'd run out of sewer pipe, Bigpaw saved the day (or so he thought) by ripping out some extra pipe he found buried in the ground.

But the pipe wasn't extra at all. It was part of the town water-main system. Water squirted in every direction. It flooded the job site. It shut off the water in every pipe, sink, and toilet in Beartown. It caused short circuits in the electrical system. Sparks flew from the overheard wires. The cry went up, "Somebody turn off the electricity!" But it was a dangerous situation. There was no way anybody

could go near the wires. Nobody except Bigpaw. He reached down and pulled two of the poles completely out of the ground. Then he raised the two poles high over his head and snapped the wires they carried. That turned off the electricity, all right. It turned it off all over Beartown. It also pulled down rows and rows of utility poles. The whole Beartown business district was a flooded tangle of downed poles and wet wire, not to mention a small army of fighting-mad businessbears. It made the disaster at Ben's farm look like tiddledywinks.

Bigpaw knew he was in trouble. He knew it even before he heard the police sirens and fire engines. Bears were up in arms all over town. Stores had to close. Elevators got stuck between floors, clocks stopped, pumps shut down. An anti-Bigpaw cry went up. "Get that monster out of town!" "He's dangerous to life and

limb!" "He can't live among ordinary folk!" "He's too strong!" "Pass a law!"

Bigpaw sat quietly on a huge stack of bricks. He felt awful. He'd messed up another job. The townsbears were right: He was just too strong. The professor and the Bear Scouts showed up and tried to console him.

Mayor Honeypot was especially angry. He was about to give an important political speech when the loudspeaker shut down. "Arrest that Pigbaw — er, Bigpaw!" cried the mayor, who sometimes got the fronts and backs of his words mixed up. "Put him in the goosehow — er, hoosegow! Cake him to tort — er, take him to court!"

And that's what happened. They took Bigpaw to the big courthouse on Main Street.

• Chapter 14 •

E-Day Minus Thirty Minutes

All was in readiness at E-Day headquarters. Dr. Boffins was up in the countdown booth doing his final calculations. Very Important Weasels were trooping in and being seated in the grandstand. The ten strongest weasels in Weaselworld stood ready to shoulder the battering ram. Chief henchweasel Stye announced the arrival of McGreed himself. Ushered in by a uniformed honor guard, McGreed was every inch the master of Weaselworld. He was wearing a red uniform trimmed in gold, a matching peaked cap, an ankle-length cloak, and a yellow-eyed sneer.

Following a drumroll, Major Kleff, director of the Weasel Marine Band, gave the downbeat and the band struck up "Hail to McGreed." All present stood and sang:

HAIL TO McGREED
MASTER OF ALL WEASELS,
EVILER THAN EVIL,
NASTIER THAN MEASLES.
THOUGH HE'S ROTTEN TO THE CORE,
HE'S OUR KING FOREVERMORE.

Stye helped McGreed onto his throne. It was a great moment for McGreed, the greatest of his life. In just thirty minutes he would achieve his lifelong goal: He would destroy Bear Country lock, stock, and honeypot.

• Chapter 15 •

A Matter of Public Safety

Of course, Bigpaw couldn't fit into the courthouse. Big as it was, it wasn't as big as Bigpaw. The professor and the scouts offered to represent him in court. Bigpaw agreed. Things didn't look good for the big fellow. There was a strong anti-Bigpaw feeling in the courtroom. It didn't help at all that the court clerk had had to put candles all around the courtroom because Bigpaw had wrecked the electricity.

"All those present honor this court, Judge Gavel presiding. All present stand!" cried the court clerk. All present stood as

Judge Gavel entered and took his place behind the bench.

"Be seated," said the judge. "I have here a petition from Mayor Honeypot and others. Court clerk, please read the petition."

"I, mayor of Beartown," read the court clerk, "request this court to put the following law into effect: From this day forward, the creature known as Bigpaw shall be banished from Beartown forever and a day!"

"All right," said the judge. "Let's hear arguments."

Bigpaw was seated on the grass in front of the courthouse. He could hear voices inside. And though he couldn't make out what was being said, he was pretty sure things were going against him.

What was going on inside the court-house was in great contrast with the peaceful scene outside the courthouse. The

courthouse itself was handsome. It had big white pillars and lots of marble steps. The scars of Bigpaw's latest job performance were a distance away and did not mar the view. Main Street was a fine wide avenue, the widest in Beartown. In front of the courthouse stood two giant oaks. Known as the Giant Twin Oaks, they were the oldest trees in Beartown. Bigpaw admired them. They were almost as big as he was. There was one on each side of the street.

Bigpaw tried to ignore the ugliness inside. But it was hard because the voices were getting angrier and angrier. A parade of witnesses had taken the stand against Bigpaw. Some were angrier than others. Mayor Honeypot got so angry that for a short time he stopped getting the fronts and backs of his words mixed up. All the witnesses agreed on one thing:

Bigpaw had to be banned from Beartown because he was *just too strong*!

"All right," said the judge, banging his gavel. "I've heard enough in favor of banning Bigpaw from Beartown. Is there anyone here to speak for the giant?"

The Bear Scouts and the professor stepped forward.

"Greetings, professor. Hello, scouts," said the judge. "Let's hear what you have to say."

The Bear Scouts did their best. They told how they had discovered Bigpaw on a fossil hunt. They explained that he was a "living fossil." They told what a gentle, sweet-natured creature he was, who wanted nothing more than a job and a chance to be useful.

The judge heard them out, but finally he said, "That's all very well, but I'm afraid it's beside the point. The case isn't about Bigpaw's character, it's about his size and strength — especially his strength. So it's really a matter of public safety that we're dealing with, and that being the case . . ."

• Chapter 16 •
E-Day: Zero Hour

"Six, five, four, three, two, one! Blast off!" cried Dr. Boffins.

The ten strongest weasels in Weasel-world started running. They ran faster and faster until they crashed the huge battering ram into the big painted X.

There was dead silence in the earth-quake room as McGreed and all present listened for the rumble that meant suc-cess. Then it came. The rumble that would mean an earthquake was being born, that would realize McGreed's fondest dream,

an earthquake that would destroy Bear Country lock, stock, and honeypot.

As the rumble turned into a roar that could only mean success, the weasels began dancing and shouting, shouting and dancing. McGreed stood on his throne, raised his arms, and cried, "All power to the weasels!"

Meanwhile, directly above the weasels was Bigpaw, still sitting on the grass, still thinking how painful it would be to be banished from Bear Country. Then something strange began to happen: The ground began to shake. The courthouse began to shake. Everything around the courthouse began to shake. Then an even stranger thing happened: The great wide street in front of the courthouse began to split open like an overripe watermelon. And the great jagged split was getting wider and longer as the shaking got worse.

Bigpaw wasn't exactly built for fast thinking. But this was an emergency. His first thought was that he would surely be blamed for it, so he took action. He straddled the widening split, locked his mighty arms around the hundred-year-old oaks, and pulled them together as hard as he could.

There followed an epic battle. It was Bigpaw versus the earthquake. First the split would get the upper hand, then Bigpaw! Then the split! Then Bigpaw! The split was the strongest thing that Bigpaw had ever gone against. But he was determined to win. He was in big enough trouble already, and he didn't want to get any more blame.

Bigpaw was so busy battling the earthquake that he didn't notice that folks had rushed out of the courthouse. They watched in awe as Bigpaw pulled the twin oaks closer, ever closer together. Finally,

Bigpaw reached back for strength he didn't even know he had and managed to close the split. The shaking stopped and gave way to a mysterious rumble. It was the sound of the earthquake going back to where it had come from. Though Dr. Boffins had studied Great Grizzly Fault

with great care, though he had done every possible calculation, he had reckoned without the gentle giant, Bigpaw.

The crowd, which was using the courthouse steps as a grandstand, fell silent. They stood in awe of what they had just seen. Then one member of the crowd cried out, "Let's hear it for Bigpaw! He just outmuscled an earthquake!" The crowd roared with appreciation. The scouts and the professor beamed with pride. Bigpaw had saved Beartown and perhaps all Bear Country from complete and total disaster.

The scouts and the professor came over to congratulate Bigpaw. "Nice going, Bigpaw!" said Brother.

"Thank you," said Bigpaw. "But Bigpaw have question. What's an earthquake?"

Another roar from the crowd, followed by a ruling from Judge Gavel. "This court rules that when it comes to earthquakes, there is no such thing as 'too strong.' Case dismissed!"

The former anti-Bigpaw crowd was now overwhelmingly pro-Bigpaw. They tried to carry Bigpaw on their shoulders. Naturally, they failed. So Bigpaw picked the crowd up on *his* shoulders and carried them down Main Street, their cheers ringing in his ears.

• Chapter 17 •

Another New Job

The bears of Beartown were grateful to Bigpaw — even Farmer Ben and Squire Grizzly. Without Bigpaw, Ben's farm and the squire's project would have been *completely* destroyed. The town council, which consisted of Mayor Honeypot, Judge Gavel, and the police chief, decided to give Bigpaw a medal. They had a beautiful one made. It said: *For Bigpaw, who outmuscled an earthquake, the grateful citizens of Beartown.*

"Thank you," said Bigpaw. "Medal very nice. But what Bigpaw really want is job."

The town council huddled briefly and offered Bigpaw a job as Director of Disaster Control. Bigpaw accepted.

And what did the Bear Scouts and the professor think about all this? They thought it was posalutely, absotively great!

FOR BIGPAW, WHO OUTMUSCLED AN EARTHQUAKE. THE GRATEFUL CITIZENS OF BEARTOWN.

• About the Authors •

Stan and Jan Berenstain have been writing and illustrating books about bears for more than thirty years. Their very first book about the Bear Scout characters was published in 1967. Through the years the Bear Scouts have done their best to defend the weak, catch the crooked, joust against the unjust, and rally against rottenness of all kinds. In fact, the scouts have done such a great job of living up to the Bear Scout Oath, the authors say, that "they deserve a series of their own."

Stan and Jan Berenstain live in Bucks County, Pennsylvania. They have two sons, Michael and Leo, and four grandchildren. Michael is an artist, and Leo is a writer. Michael did the pictures in this book.

Don't Miss

THE *Berenstain* BEAR SCOUTS

Scream Their Heads Off

All four scouts followed Jane upstairs, not because they had any desire to check out the ghostly wail but because they were terrified of being left behind. Inching their way up the long dark stairway wasn't exactly the most fun they had ever had. Halfway up they found their path blocked by a huge cobweb with a big black spider in its center. The ugly creature was so big that it looked like a hairy black hand with long curved fingers. Scout Leader Jane bravely used her flashlight as a club to knock away the web and its terrifying weaver. Meanwhile, the ghostly wail came closer and closer as they climbed. "WHO-O-O-O-O!"

Finally, they reached the top of the stairs and followed the sound to a closed door. Jane took hold of the doorknob. "Ready, scouts?" she said. "Here goes . . ."

Jane flung open the door, and they all shined their flashlights into the room. What they saw made their knees knock together.

"It's a g-g-*ghost*!" shrieked Sister.

They all screamed at the top of their lungs.